Joseph Trowbridge Bailey

Ancestry of Joseph Trowbridge Bailey

of Philadelphia and Catherine Goddard Weaver of Newport, Rhode Island

Joseph Trowbridge Bailey

Ancestry of Joseph Trowbridge Bailey
of Philadelphia and Catherine Goddard Weaver of Newport, Rhode Island

ISBN/EAN: 9783337378356

Printed in Europe, USA, Canada, Australia, Japan

Cover: Foto ©Andreas Hilbeck / pixelio.de

More available books at **www.hansebooks.com**

ANCESTRY

OF

JOSEPH TROWBRIDGE BAILEY[2]

OF PHILADELPHIA

AND

CATHERINE GODDARD WEAVER[2]

OF NEWPORT, RHODE ISLAND.

BY

JOSEPH TROWBRIDGE BAILEY [2]

PRINTED PRIVATELY
PHILADELPHIA
1892

INTRODUCTION.

During many years I have at intervals made researches among all the trustworthy documents procurable connected with the history of my family, and have obtained a record so complete that I desire to put it into a shape which will insure its preservation.

It is not my intention to give this book to the general public; the distribution of the few copies which I shall have printed will be confined to my children, my relatives, and my most intimate friends.

I was led to commence and carry on the work by various reasons, any one of which appears to me cogent enough to justify the expenditure of time and trouble which the undertaking has involved.

It is natural and right for a man to wish to learn as much as possible in regard to the lives and characters of those through whom the name he bears has been transmitted generation after generation. During the past quarter of a century science has demonstrated clearly the powerful influence which heredity exerts on races and on individuals, and we have learned that it is only through a knowledge of our predecessors that we can fairly judge either ourselves or those connected with us by ties of blood.

The importance of such knowledge to parents must be evident to every thinking person, since by its light they can not only guard against any signs of transmitted physical weakness, but can understandingly combat undesirable mental or moral peculiarities. Children so early develop prominent traits of character that inherited defects are soon recognizable, and by constant care and judicious training these can usually be prevented from becoming so powerful that in later life they will overmaster better and higher qualities, as neglected weeds choke and root out the fairest flowers of a garden.

One inducement I have had in undertaking this record is the fact that I hold myself specially fortunate in my ancestors, and feel, as any one ought to do, a pride and an incentive in the fact that through both my father and my mother I descended from a line of men and women whose careers were honorable and whose lives were valuable in their day and generation.

The men, like all the early settlers of this country, endured hardships and passed through trials which we at this distance of time can with difficulty realize; but they were faithful in the discharge of private and public duties, painstaking, earnest, honest, and upright. The women were helpmeets in the highest sense of the word: faithful wives and mothers, and useful and influential members of society.

Still another inducement—the one closest to my heart of all—urged me to begin my work: a reason well known to my relatives and friends, yet in regard to which I cannot forbear adding a few words.

As I grow older and more reflective, I contemplate with an ever increasing veneration the character of my father in the splendor of its integrity and manliness, and do still deeper homage to the sweetness and purity of my mother's nature. Filial duty and affection alike impel me to perpetuate my knowledge of these parents, in order that my descendants may learn to appreciate their virtues and emulate their example.

It only remains for me to add that the genealogies and personal memorials in this volume are compiled from official or other thoroughly authenticated sources, such as wills, genealogical works, and family Bibles.

The lists contain the complete and proven lineage of five lines in direct descent of my paternal and maternal families, viz.:

> *Benoni Bailey,   from the year 1697*
> *Thomas Benedict,   "   "   "   1617*
> *Robert Potter,   about the year 1600*
> *John Green,   "   "   "   1599*
> *Richard Raymond, "   "   "   1602*

To these are added five successive lines of my wife's family, viz.:

> *Clement Weaver,   from about 1596*
> *William Spooner, from the year 1637*
> *John Briggs,   ."   "   "   1648*
> *John Coggeshall,   about 1591*
> *William Freeborn,   about 1600*

All the descendants of the Baileys of Danbury, Conn., who have ever resided in Philadelphia are mentioned in this volume. These families alone can claim relationship with the Baileys of Danbury, Conn., and consequently no other persons of the name residing in Philadelphia are connected with any branch of my family. The only descendants of the Weavers of Newport, Rhode Island, who have ever resided in Philadelphia are Catherine Goddard Weaver (2) and Clement Weaver and his son and daughter.

I find that reliable records are in existence of most of the collateral lines of descent of both the Baileys and Weavers, and I have reason to believe that the pedigrees of all could be as clearly and unbrokenly traced as these here collected.

JOSEPH TROWBRIDGE BAILEY (2).

THE BAILEYS

Great-great-great-grandfather.

BENONI BAILEY, born 1697, died May, 1793, at Danbury, Connecticut, aged 96 years.

Great-great-grandfather.

SAMUEL, born 1728, died March, 1808, at Danbury, aged 80 years.

Great-grandfather.

BENJAMIN, born December 9, 1756, died June 21, 1807; married HANNAH DIBBLE, born February 10, 1761, died November 6, 1800, both of Danbury.

Grandfather.

MAJOR BAILEY, born May 21, 1783, died January 23, 1833, married November 24, 1804, LUCY BENEDICT, born June 23, 1786, died January, 1872, both of Danbury.

Father.

JOSEPH TROWBRIDGE BAILEY (I), born December 16, 1806, died March 13, 1854, married in Philadelphia, June 21, 1834, by Rt. Rev. William White, Episcopal Bishop of Pennsylvania, MARY POTTER, daughter of SHELDON and SARAH BETSY (RAYMOND) POTTER, born December 9, 1811, died March 8, 1841.

5

JOSEPH TROWBRIDGE (1) and MARY (POTTER) BAILEY had two children : JOSEPH TROWBRIDGE (2), born March 29, 1835 ; EMILY (1), born May 8, 1839, both born in Philadelphia.

JOSEPH TROWBRIDGE (2), only son of JOSEPH TROWBRIDGE (1) and MARY (POTTER) BAILEY, married September 1, 1857, in Old Trinity Church at Newport, Rhode Island, by the Rt. Rev. Alonzo Potter, Episcopal Bishop of Pennsylvania, CATHERINE GODDARD WEAVER (2), born in Newport, Rhode Island, March 21, 1835, daughter of JOSEPH B. WEAVER and ABBY (MARSH) WEAVER, of Newport, Rhode Island.

EMILY (1), only daughter of JOSEPH TROWBRIDGE (1) and MARY (POTTER) BAILEY, married first, November 5, 1857, HENRY HARRISON, died February 13, 1860, of Newark, New Jersey; married second, CHARLES DUGGIN, of New-York, on April 15, 1862.

No children.

JOSEPH TROWBRIDGE (2) and CATHERINE GODDARD (WEAVER) (2) BAILEY have four children : EMILIE (2), born November 29, 1858, at Philadelphia; JOSEPH TROWBRIDGE (3), born June 15, 1860, at Newport, Rhode Island; CHARLES WEAVER, born October 20, 1861, at Philadelphia; KATHRYN LOUIS, born May 28, 1871, at Philadelphia.

EMILIE (2), eldest daughter, married first, on December 5, 1878, at St. Mary's Church, West Philadelphia, HENRY AUGUSTUS BURROUGHS,* born March 10, 1856, died March 1, 1882, son of HORATIO NELSON (1) and CAROLINE BURROUGHS, of Philadelphia. They had one son, HORATIO NELSON (2), born December 17, 1879. Second marriage on February 13, 1884, to EDMUND BRANDT AYMAR* (2),

* Appendix.

of New-York, born September 7, 1858, son of EDMUND BRANDT (1)
and ELEANOR KINGSLAND (CLARK) AYMAR, of New-York.

Their children.

ELEANOR, born November 14, 1884.
EDMUND BRANDT (3), born July 3, 1887.

JOSEPH TROWBRIDGE (3), eldest son, married on January 18, 1888,
at Stamford, Connecticut, AMY THOMSON,* born in Philadelphia
October 12, 1862, the daughter of ALEXANDER HAMILTON THOM-
SON and CAROLINE MACKEY WHITE, both of Philadelphia.

CHARLES WEAVER, second son, married April 9, 1884, ANNE, daughter of ANDREW JACKSON SLOAN and MARY WILSON POTTER, of
Philadelphia.

Their children.

EMILIE (3) AYMAR, born April 20, 1887.
BEATRICE, born March 1, 1892.

KATHRYN LOUIS, youngest daughter, married December 15, 1890, in
Philadelphia, by the Rt. Rev. Henry C. Potter, Episcopal Bishop of
New-York, and Hon. Edwin H. Fitler, Mayor of Philadelphia, JEAN
THEODULE FRANCISQUE LOUIS, Comte de Sibour,* born March 19,
1865, son of JEAN ANTONIN GABRIEL, Vicomte, and MARIE LOUISE,
Vicomtesse de Sibour, of Paris and Carpentras, France.

Their son.

LOUIS BLAISE DE SIBOUR, Vicomte,
born in Paris, France, December 26, 1891.

* Appendix.

2

THE BAILEYS

OF DANBURY, CONNECTICUT, AND PHILADELPHIA.

AMONGST the earliest settlers of Jamaica, Long Island, appears the name of John Bailey, often termed Goodman Bailey, who arrived from England about the same date, if he was not of that company of Puritans which, under the leadership of Rev. Richard Denton, emigrated from Hemstead, England, in the early part of the 17th century, landed on the shores of Connecticut, and subsequently settled Long Island. John Bailey's name appears prominently in the island records of settlement and enterprise, and with it frequently occurs that of Thomas Benedict.

The names of Benedict and Bailey have been closely associated for 250 years. The traditions of the family, as well as the researches which I have made, justify the belief that Benoni Bailey, my great-great-great-grandfather, was the grandson or great-grandson of John Bailey of Jamaica, Long Island, the friend of Thomas Benedict (1), also of Jamaica and Southold. Thomas Benedict removed from Long Island and founded Danbury, Connecticut; at an early age Benoni Bailey is also found living in that town and associated with the Benedict family. My grandmother Lucy (Benedict) Bailey, who died in 1872, aged 86 years, told me that the Baileys' ancestor first landed in Connecticut and then removed to Long Island, and that Benoni Bailey had come to Connecticut from Long Island.

The fact that John Bailey landed first in Connecticut and removed to Long Island, and was an early settler, is published in severa' Colonial histories, and it may therefore be inferred that Benoni w.. descended from John, who was probably his grandfather.

JOSEPH TROWBRIDGE BAILEY [1]

AT THE AGE OF 41 YEARS.

FROM A MINIATURE BY J. HENRY BROWN

The fully authenticated records of the Baileys date back to Benoni, who was born in 1696. He resided a mile or two from the little village of Bethel, situated on the borders of Danbury. His farm was close to, if it did not join, that of the members of the Benedict family. In his will, probated at Fairfield, Connecticut, at the time of his death, which took place in May, 1792, he bequeathed his lands to his children, using the primitive names given the sections by the early settlers. One tract was called Wolf Pits, and we know that another section was named Wild Cats. He lived to the ripe age of 96, and died on "Training Day." He was buried in the old Bethel burial-ground at the back of the church, and the inscription on his tombstone was still visible a few years ago.

Samuel Bailey, my great-great-grandfather, born in 1728, resided in the same place, as did also his son, Benjamin Bailey, born December 9, 1756. They were farmers, and for 150 years their descendants occupied the old homestead at Stony Hill, several miles from Danbury, Connecticut, and almost adjoining the little village of Bethel.

The records of the family other than the will of Benoni and the old family Bible are unfortunately few. When the British troops under General Tryon made their raid on Connecticut, in April, 1777, they burned the Bethel Church, in which were preserved the registers of the marriages and deaths of all the Baileys since 1696, and these were completely destroyed. The family Bible is, however, an invaluable record. This Bible, which has descended to me from my great-grandfather, Benjamin Bailey, contains the accounts of all the births from that of Benoni Bailey, in 1696, to my own in 1835. The book has been transmitted by the successive heads of the family, and the writing is in many different hands.

Major Bailey, my grandfather, son of Benjamin, was born in Danbury, and married there Lucy Benedict, the great-great-great-granddaughter of Thomas Benedict, the original settler, who was my great-great-great-great-great-grandfather. Shortly after his marriage, Major Bailey removed to Thompson, New-York, and afterward to Pough-keepsie, where he resided for many years, going from thence to the city of New-York.

Joseph Trowbridge (1), his son, has written the following in the old family Bible concerning his father's demise, which occurred in New-York City: " His death was caused by an injury from a fall on board of the brig *Evelina* on September 10, 1832, from which time he lingered until his death, exhibiting in a wonderful degree that patience and resignation for which he was always characterized. His mental faculties remained unimpaired to the last, which gave him abundant time for reflection and to fully express his feelings and sentiments in regard to his approaching end. At peace with God and his own conscience, and in full assurance of meeting us all in heaven, he was led to exclaim, ' But for the parting with you, my wife and children, death has no terrors for me.' He died January 3, 1833."

PARENTS.

My father, Joseph Trowbridge Bailey (1), was born in Thompson, New-York, a year after the removal of his parents to that town from Danbury, Connecticut. Later a new home was made in Poughkeepsie, where my father passed his childhood and early youth. When he was twenty-one years old he established himself in Philadelphia, and by his own talent and energy built up a large and successful business.

It was here that he first saw Mary Potter, and their acquaintance speedily ripened into an affection which became henceforth the leading influence in both lives. Their union took place on June 21, 1834, and proved one of exceptional happiness; the only shadow which ever touched its brightness being caused by the delicacy of my mother's health. This misfortune was due to an accident she met with in early girlhood, the effects of which were indeed the ultimate cause of her death.

My father was a man of singularly strong intellect and education, and circumstances early developed his reason and ripened his judgment to a maturity which few men reach before middle age.

His prosperous and happy life came to a premature end when he was in the prime of his mental and physical powers. At the age of forty-eight he died suddenly in Matanzas, Cuba, to which place he had been sent by his physicians on account of his health.

The Cuban authorities forbade the removal of the body; but, through the interposition of influential friends, Captain John Gallagher, the commander of a vessel which ran between Philadelphia and Matanzas, undertook to procure the remains and transmit them to the family.

In the dead of night a boat conveyed several of the ship's crew to the shore; the coffin was exhumed and carried on board the vessel, which immediately set sail on its return voyage.

Few men have been so deeply regretted as was my father by a large circle of relatives and friends, whose unanimous verdict fully bears out my own lofty estimate of his character.

His whole life was marked by a conscientiousness ·which had its source in the very well-springs of his being, so strong that it permeated every thought and directed every action, making the basis of a sympathy for others which knew no bounds, and inspiring a patience which never faltered, a charity which never failed.

His mind was at once broad and acute, eminently logical and peculiarly luminous. He was an earnest student from boyhood, and possessed a range of information as deep as it was wide and varied, which, with the aids of a ready wit and a remarkable control of language, rendered him an exceptionally brilliant conversationalist.

He was so close a reasoner, and so quick to perceive every side of a subject, that in argument he was nearly invincible, and he possessed a self-control which never deserted him in the height of the most heated debate.

A wonderful force of will and an unfailing presence of mind greatly aided in rendering his career prosperous. Whatever crisis might arrive, his indomitable will rose undauntedly to meet it, and provided him with the exact remedy needed, no matter how sudden the necessity or how menacing the emergency.

In his domestic and social relations the finest and sweetest qualities of his nature had free play: he was a devoted husband, a tender parent, a faithful friend. By all who knew him intimately his counsel was deemed invaluable, his deliberate opinions a sure guide, his blame just as the accusation of conscience, and his approval a bulwark of strength.

It would be difficult to overrate the influence of a life so exalted in its ideal, so consistent in its practice, so noble in every detail; for that influence does not perish when the life ends: it survives to enlighten and encourage those who come after, to be at once a model and a support.

My mother died before I was old enough to comprehend the full force of her loss; but the lapse of years has not dimmed the remembrance of her beautiful presence, which was the light of her household and the admiration of the outside world.

From her friends I have received enthusiastic assurances of the respect and love gained by her personal beauty, her grace of manner, and the sweetness of her disposition, gifts to which were added numerous accomplishments, rare musical talent, and the discriminating appreciation of books taught by extensive and well-directed reading.

The inscription which my father placed on her tomb well expressed the sentiment of the many who with him mourned her untimely loss:

" Torn from us in thy loveliness,
    Thy unspotted life, hallowed by
    The charms of thy exalted virtue,
    Lives in the memory of all who knew thee,
    Cherished — never to die."

To make the characters of my parents fully understood and appreciated by my children has always been prominent in my mind, and it is a source of unfailing happiness to me to feel certain that they in turn will teach their sons and daughters to venerate the memories of that noble pair.

THE BENEDICTS

Great-great-great-great-great-grandfather.

THOMAS BENEDICT (1), born 1617, died 1690, married about 1640 MARY BRIDGUM, who lived to be 100 years old.

Great-great-great-great-grandfather.

JAMES (2), born 164–, survived certainly until August, 1717, married May 10, 1676, SARAH GREGORY, born December, 1652.

Great-great-great-grandfather.

THOMAS (3), born November 9, 1694, died July, 1776, married ABIGAIL HOYT, daughter of JOHN HOYT, one of the original settlers of Danbury, Connecticut.

Great-great-grandfather.

THOMAS (4), born 1727, died November 14, 1821, married MERCY KNAPP, born 1727, died May 15, 1811.

Great-grandfather.

JOSHUA (5), born April 2, 1753, died March 16, 1825, at Poughkeepsie, New-York, married April 13, 1774, RUTH, daughter of NATHANIEL WESCOTT, of Norwalk, Connecticut, born April 19, 1753, died August 16, 1838, at Poughkeepsie, New-York.

14

Grandmother.

LUCY, born June 23, 1786, died January, 1872, married November, 1805, MAJOR BAILEY, born May 21, 1783, died January 23, 1833.

Father.

JOSEPH TROWBRIDGE BAILEY (1), born December 16, 1806, died March 13, 1854, married June 21, 1834, MARY POTTER, born December 9, 1811, died March 8, 1841.

Their children.

JOSEPH TROWBRIDGE BAILEY (2), born March 29, 1835; EMILY BAILEY (1), born May 8, 1839.

THE BENEDICTS

OF DANBURY, CONNECTICUT.

THOMAS BENEDICT, my great-great-great-great-great-grandfather, was born in 1617, at Nottinghamshire. He came to New England in 1638, in the same vessel with his future wife, Mary Bridgum, who lived to the age of 100 years. The pair were married and settled in Massachusetts Bay, but subsequently removed to Long Island, where they resided at Southold.

The commissioners of the United Colonies of New England appointed Thomas Benedict to adjust differences between Uncas, the Sachem of the Mohegans, and Mohansick, Sachem of Long Island; date of his appointment, September 5, 1650. May, 1658, he was one of the petitioners to have the town of Huntingdon annexed to New Haven. Appointed by the General Court, May 15, 1662, as Commissioner of his town. On March 20, 1663, appointed Magistrate by the Dutch Governor Stuyvesant. At this time he resided at Jamaica, Long Island. September 29, 1663, was one of the petitioners to the General Court of Connecticut, to annex Long Island, and appointed Lieutenant of the town, December 3, 1663.

September 26, 1664, Thomas Benedict, with three or four others, received a grant to settle Elizabeth City, State of New Jersey. Grant signed by Sir Richard Nicolls, Governor of New-York. This place is now Elizabeth, New Jersey.

In 1665 Governor Nicolls issued an order for a general meeting from each town. Thomas Benedict was one of two delegates from Jamaica, Long Island. This is said to have been the first English legislative body convened in New-York.

In 1665 he was appointed Lieutenant of the Foot Company of Jamaica. Later he removed to Norwalk, Connecticut, and was Selectman and Town Clerk until 1674, and Selectman till 1688. His name is one of the forty-two comprising the list of freemen of Norwalk in 1669. In 1669 he was Representative of Norwalk in the General Assembly, again in 1670 and 1675. Was a patentee on the title of Norwalk, in 1686. In 1684 the General Court appointed him with three others to make a settlement near Norwalk. This they did in the autumn of 1684 and spring of 1685, and settled there permanently. The land was purchased from the Indians. This is Danbury, Connecticut.

He was one of the most prominent men in public affairs in his section of the country, and this is only a brief extract from the voluminous records of his services.

He was one of the founders of the first Presbyterian church ever erected in America, built at Jamaica, Long Island, in 1662, and his name appears upon the records of that church as Goodman Thomas Benedict.

James Benedict, my great-great-great-great-grandfather, was one of the eight who purchased and settled Danbury, Connecticut, having sold his property in Norwalk, on March 26, 1691.

His son Thomas, my great-great-great-grandfather, was also one of the original settlers of Danbury.   In May, 1738, he was appointed Justice of the Peace and first Judge of the District, and he held both offices until his death, which occurred on the 4th of July, 1776.   He was also a member of the Connecticut Legislature for thirty-one sessions, between May, 1737, and October, 1766, inclusive.

His son Thomas, my great-great-grandfather, also resided in Danbury, and possibly was a Selectman in 1785.

Joshua, his son and my great-grandfather, was born and resided in Danbury, and died in Poughkeepsie, New-York State, in 1825.   He was appointed to supply horse-trappings for the artillery and cavalry during the Revolutionary War.   He related to my uncle, Mr. Eli Westcott Bailey,* when the latter was a boy, the exciting incidents through which he passed, the difficulty he had to procure the necessary outfits, and told how he was obliged to accompany squads of men into the forest for days at a time, to select and cut the natural crooks from trees which would be suitable for good saddle-trees.   He was living at Danbury when that town was attacked and burnt by the British troops, on Sunday morning, April 27, 1777.   His house, with those of the other members of his family, was marked for destruction by the resident Tories of the town.   Five of the nineteen houses burnt by the British belonged to the Benedicts.   He removed his young children in great haste in order to escape capture, and secreted them several miles distant, at a place called Stony Hill.

* Appendix.

My great-great-great-uncle Captain Elisha Benedict was born in Danbury on April 2, 1736.   In 1774 he was engaged by the direction of the New-York Provincial Congress to form military companies in Cumberland County, Vermont.   On June 29, 1775, he was commissioned Captain in the Eighth Company of the 2d New-York Continental Regiment, and served before Quebec in 1776.

In October, 1780, Elisha and his three sons, Ensign Caleb, Elias, and Felix, and his negro servant, were surprised in their beds and taken prisoners by the British and Indians under Major Monroe.   They all fell to the lot of Captain John, the leader of the Indians, and were carried to Canada.   The pay-roll of sundry officers, on file in the office of the Comptroller of the State of New-York, shows that Captain Elisha, Elias, and Felix were kept prisoners two and a half years.   Elisha died August 26, 1798.

My great-great-great-uncle Robert Benedict was born in 1744, and was a Commissary in the Revolution.   Died in 1828.

My great-great-great-uncle Thaddeus was Justice of the Peace of Danbury from 1774 to 1800, and a Selectman in 1784.   He was one of the sufferers by the burning of Danbury in 1777, and was allowed by the State, May, 1792, five hundred and twenty-one pounds, nineteen shillings and sixpence for his losses.   He died on January 20, 1805.

My grandmother Lucy (Benedict) Bailey, the daughter of Joshua, was born in Danbury 1786, and married my grandfather Major Bailey, also of Danbury, in November, 1805.   On the death of Major Bailey she removed to Philadelphia, where she resided with my father, Joseph Trowbridge Bailey (1), for many years ; she died in January, 1872, aged eighty-six years, and was buried in the family lot in Laurel Hill Cemetery.

MARY POTTER BAILEY,

AT THE AGE OF ? YEARS.

FROM A MINIATURE BY THOMAS OFFELER

THE POTTERS

Great-great-great-great-great-great-grandfather.

ROBERT POTTER, died 1655, married ISABEL ——, died 1643.

Great-great-great-great-great-grandfather.

JOHN (1), born 1639, died 1694, married June 2, 1669, RUTH FISHER.

Great-great-great-great-grandfather.

JOHN (2), born November 21, 1669, died February 5, 1711, married JANE BURLINGHAM.

Great-great-great-grandfather.

JOHN (3), born before 1695, married December 12, 1717, PHEBE GREEN, born May 10, 1693.

Great-great-grandfather.

THOMAS, born March 25, 1735, died November 13, 1795, married October 16, 1755, ESTHER SHELDON, born 1738, died 1800.

Great-grandfather.

JOSEPH, born August 12, 1757, died November 23, 1824, married December 27, 1781, ANNE KNIGHT, born February 10, 1760, died April 28, 1833.

Grandfather.

SHELDON, born April 19, 1789, died February 1, 1834, married
February 28, 1811, SARAH BETSY RAYMOND, born August 27,
1792, died April 24, 1872.

Mother.

MARY, born December 9, 1811, died March 8, 1841, married June 21,
1834, JOSEPH TROWBRIDGE BAILEY (1), born December 16, 1806,
died March 13, 1854.

Their children.

JOSEPH TROWBRIDGE BAILEY (2), born March 29, 1835; EMILY
BAILEY (1), born May 8, 1839.

THE POTTERS

OF WARWICK, RHODE ISLAND.

MY great-great-great-great-great-great-grandfather Robert Potter
came from Coventry, England, in 1634, and was made a freeman of
the Massachusetts Plantation on September 3, 1634. He first resided
at Lynn, Massachusetts, and afterward at Roxbury. He was a fol-
lower of Samuel Gorton, the great religious disturber, and they,
together with their associates, purchased land known as the "Shaw-
omett Purchase," in Rhode Island, and founded a town which they
named Warwick, in honor of the Earl of Warwick, who had befriended
them in their troubles with the Plantation of Massachusetts. The deed
from the Indian Sachem "Miantonomy," drawn on January 12, 1642,
was made out to Robert Potter and others for the ground upon which
the town of Warwick now stands.

In 1638 Robert was admitted as an inhabitant of the island of Aquidneck, Rhode Island. In 1639 he, and twenty-eight others, signed a compact acknowledging themselves the legal subjects of his Majesty King Charles.

Gorton, Robert Potter, and their associates were religious agitators. They agreed with the Quakers in some points, but differed from them in others.

On account of their religious opinions they were disfranchised by the colony of Rhode Island from all privileges in 1642, and were ordered to leave the colony.

In 1643 Robert Potter and the other members of the colony were notified to appear before a General Court in Boston to answer in regard to some dispute with the Indians.   As they declined to obey the order, Captain Cook was sent from Boston with a company of soldiers, and besieged them in a fortified house.   In the parley which ensued, it was stated " that they held blasphemous errors which they must repent of," or go to Boston for trial. They were carried to Boston and imprisoned, and their wives and children were forced to betake themselves to the woods for concealment, and were cared for by the Indians, suffering such hardships that three of the women died, one of them being my great-great-great-great-great-great-grandmother Isabel, wife of Robert.

On the 3d day of September, 1643, sentence was passed upon the settlers that in case they continued their blasphemous and abominable heresies, either in writing, publishing, declaring, or maintaining such abominations, they should be condemned to death and executed. Their lives were spared after much hesitation, but they were imprisoned and put in irons, which punishment created much sympathy and discontent among the inhabitants.

In 1646 an order was promulgated by the Commissioners of Foreign Plantations in England reinstating the prisoners in their rights, giving

them possession of Warwick, and forbidding the Colony of Massachusetts to molest them in any manner.   The Rev. Nathaniel Ward, who
held a conversation with Robert concerning his religious belief whilst
the latter was a prisoner at Boston, evidently considered him a very
sinful man on account of his new opinions, and spoke of Samuel Gorton
as "Starke drunke with Blasphemies and insolencies, a corrupter of the
truth and the disturber of the Peace wherever hee comes."

John Potter (1), his son, my great-great-great-great-great-grand-
father, was enrolled a freeman in 1660.   He was married to Ruth
Fisher by Mayor John Greene, afterward the Deputy Governor of
Rhode Island, who was also my great-great-great-great-great-grand-
father.   John Potter was Deputy 1667 to 1683, member of Court
Martial on trial of Indians August 24, 1676, Assistant 1685 and 1686.

John (2), my great-great-great-great-grandfather, born in Warwick
in 1669, was killed by the falling of a tree on February 5, 1711.

John (3), my great-great-great-grandfather, was born before 1695,
and lived on the Rivulet Farm, one mile from the Quaker Meeting-
house in Cranston, Rhode Island.   The house in which he resided was
built by his grandfather John (1), born in 1639.   He was married by
Richard Waterman, Justice of the Peace, on December 12, 1717, to
Phebe Greene, the daughter of Thomas Greene (3) and Ann (Greene)
Greene, who were cousins.   It is through my great-great-great-grandmother Phebe (Greene) Potter that I am related to the Greenes of
Rhode Island.

Thomas, my great-great-grandfather, who married Esther Sheldon,
left no records.

Joseph Potter, my great-grandfather, son of John (3), was a farmer; he and his wife belonged to the Society of Friends. He represented his county in the State Legislature of New-York, and removed from Rhode Island, in 1792, to Beekman, now La Grange, State of New-York, where he resided till his death.

Sheldon Potter, my grandfather, son of Joseph, was born at La Grange, New-York, twelve miles from Poughkeepsie. At an early age he developed a taste for literature, and on his removal to Philadelphia became a publisher. He possessed a remarkably fine physique, engaging social qualities, a high moral character, and was the companion of the leading intellectual men of the city.

His brother, the Rt. Rev. Alonzo Potter, my great-uncle, was Bishop of the Protestant Episcopal Church of the Diocese of Pennsylvania. An interesting biography of his life has been written by Dr. N. A. De Witt Howe. The Rt. Rev. Horatio Potter, also my great-uncle, was Sixth Bishop of the Protestant Episcopal Church of the Diocese of New-York. A beautiful obituary of Bishop Horatio Potter is published in "The Potter Families, and their Descendants in America."

The Rt. Rev. Henry C. Potter, present Episcopal Bishop of New-York, is my second cousin.

THE GREENES

Great-great-great-great-great-great-grandfather.

JOHN GREENE (1), born 1597, died 1658, married November 4, 1619, JOAN TATTERSALL.

His son.
Great-great-great-great-great-grandfather.

THOMAS GREENE (2), born 1628, died June 5, 1717, married June 30, 1659, ELIZABETH BARTON, died August 20, 1693.

His son.
Great-great-great-great-grandfather.

THOMAS GREENE (3), born August 14, 1662, married his cousin.

Great-great-great-great-great-grandfather.

JOHN GREENE (2), son of John Greene (1), known as Deputy Governor, born in England 1620, died November 27, 1708, aged 88 years, married ANN ALMY, born 1627, died May 17, 1709, aged 88 years.

His daughter.
Great-great-great-great-grandmother.

ANN GREENE, born March 19, 1663, died August, 1693, married her cousin.

24

THOMAS GREENE (3), son of THOMAS (2), married his cousin ANN (GREENE) GREENE, daughter of JOHN GREENE, Deputy Governor of State of Rhode Island.

Their daughter.
Great-great-great-grandmother.

PHEBE GREENE, born Wednesday, May 10, 1693, married December 12, 1717, JOHN POTTER (3), born before 1695.

Great-great-grandfather.

THOMAS POTTER, born March 25, 1735, died November 13, 1795, married October 16, 1755, ESTHER SHELDON, born 1738, died 1800.

Great-grandfather.

JOSEPH POTTER, born August 12, 1757, died November 23, 1824, married December 27, 1781, ANNE KNIGHT, born February 10, 1760, died April 28, 1833.

Grandfather.

SHELDON POTTER, born April 19, 1789, died February 1, 1834, married February 28, 1811, SARAH BETSY RAYMOND, born August 27, 1792, died April 24, 1872.

Mother.

MARY POTTER, born December 9, 1811, died March 8, 1841, married June 21, 1834, JOSEPH TROWBRIDGE BAILEY (1), born December 16, 1806, died March 13, 1854.

Their children.

JOSEPH TROWBRIDGE BAILEY (2), born March 29, 1835; EMILY BAILEY, born May 8, 1839.

THE GREENES

OF WARWICK, RHODE ISLAND.

JOHN GREENE, surgeon, my great-great-great-great-great-great-grandfather, was the son of Peter, of Aukley Hall, Salisbury, Wiltshire, England.   He was born about 1597, at Browridge Hall, Gillingham, England, where his father, grandfather, and great-grandfather, Richard, Richard, and Robert, had resided.   His family dates back to the 15th century.

George Washington Greene, in his " Life of Major-General Nathaniel Greene," states that John came over in the next company after Roger Williams, and with his wife and children followed Roger Williams to Providence, Rhode Island.   He sailed from England in the ship *James* April 6, 1635, and arrived in Boston June 5, 1635.   John Greene was one of the twelve persons to whom Roger Williams deeded land bought from the Indian Sachems " Canonicus " and " Miantonomy" in 1638. In 1643 he, with ten others, bought from the Sachem " Miantonomy" the land on which is now situated the town of Warwick, Rhode Island, of which he was one of the original founders.

Himself and others were dissenters from the prevailing religion, and held " blasphemous errors which they were required to go to Boston and repent of."

In 1644 he and Samuel Gorton, the great religious agitator, went to England, to obtain redress for their wrongs, and in 1646 they returned, having been successful in their efforts.   From 1654 to 1657 he was Commissioner.   John Greene died in 1658.

His oldest son, John Greene (2), my great-great-great-great-great-grandfather, was Deputy Governor of Rhode Island ; he was born in

1620, and died November 27, 1708, aged 88 years. His name first appears in public in 1642, as a witness to the purchase of lands from the Indians on which the town of Warwick is now located.

In 1651 he was elected Commissioner from Warwick, and occupied that office until 1658. He was then elected Assistant, and continued yearly, with two exceptions, in that office until 1686. He was again elected Assistant in 1689, and in 1690 was made Deputy Governor of the State of Rhode Island, which position he held until 1700, a period of ten years. In "The Greenes of Warwick" it is stated that he was Governor a longer time than any other person who occupied that position continuously in colonial government except Governor Cranston of Rhode Island. In 1651 and 1652 he was Recorder, and appointed in 1657, 1658, and 1659 Attorney-General. He was one of the Committee in 1654 to revise the laws. In 1664 he was also on the Commission for the same purpose with Roger Williams.

In the session of the Rhode Island Assembly of June 29, 1670, he was appointed to go to England to vindicate the charter before the king. From 1683 to the time of Andros he held a commission in the army of Major of The Main, equivalent to the present rank of a major-general of the United States army.

October, 1664, he was one of the Commission to meet Commissioners from Connecticut to settle the boundary lines between Connecticut and Rhode Island, and again on the same commission in 1670. On March 13, 1676, was invited, with sixteen other prominent citizens, to attend the session of Assembly to "advise in these troublesome times and straites."

In 1671 he was again commissioned with others to settle differences with Connecticut. In 1666 he was appointed with others to draw up an address to his Majesty and the Lord Chancellor of England. Again on a committee in 1671, to draw up an answer to the Governor of

Plymouth, Massachusetts. In 1664 he was one of the two Rhode Island Commissioners to make a treaty with Massachusetts.

In 1686 he was notified by Governor Andros of his appointment as a member of his council. In 1690 he, with others, sent a letter of congratulations to William and Mary on their accession to the crown.

The records of his public services for fifty years teem with the evidences of the esteem in which John Greene was held by his associates and the public.

A work called "The Greenes of Warwick," to be found in any State Historical Society library, contains a full account of my ancestors on the side of the Greenes in colonial and revolutionary days. In this connection I must note that the great-great-grandfather of Nathaniel Greene, Major-General, War of the Revolution, was Thomas Greene, my great-great-great-great-great-grandfather. The descent is clearly traced in the "Life of Major-General Nathaniel Greene," by George Washington Greene. Appendix, first volume.

THE RAYMONDS

Great-great-great-great-great-grandfather.

RICHARD RAYMOND (1), died at Saybrook, aged 90 years, in 1692, married JUDITH

Either his great-grandson or his great-great-grandson was my
Great-great-grandfather.

CAPTAIN CLAPP (1) RAYMOND, born 1730, married REBECCA BETTS, born 1735, died April 9, 1811.

Great-grandfather.

CLAPP (2), born June 20, 1765, died May 16, 1831, married February 1, 1787, SARAH DUNNING, died January 4, 1831, aged 64 years.

Grandmother.

SARAH BETSY, born August 27, 1792, died April 24, 1872, married February 28, 1811, SHELDON POTTER, born April 19, 1789, died February 1, 1834.

Mother.

MARY POTTER, born December 9, 1811, died March 8, 1841, married June 21, 1834, JOSEPH TROWBRIDGE BAILEY (1), born December 16, 1806, died March 13, 1854.

Their children.

JOSEPH TROWBRIDGE BAILEY (2), born March 29, 1835; EMILY
BAILEY (1), born May 8, 1839.

THE RAYMONDS

OF NORWALK, CONNECTICUT.

RICHARD RAYMOND, the first of the family in New England, arrived
about 1632, and settled at Salem, Massachusetts.   He was a freeman
on May 14, 1634.   On January 2, 1636, the town granted him half
an acre of land at Winter Harbor.   In 1636 he received a further grant
of sixty acres at Jeffries Creek, now Manchester.   He appears to have
been a sea-captain ; he was engaged in the coastwise trade with the
Dutch and English settlers on Manhattan Island, and mention is made
of his disposing of a share of a vessel.   In 1662 he moved to Norwalk,
Connecticut, and purchased land.   In 1664 he removed to Saybrook.
He and his wife Judith were members of the First Church of Salem
before 1636, and their children were baptized there.

Captain Clapp Raymond was the grandson or great-grandson of
Richard.   He was born in 1730, and married Rebecca Betts, of Norwalk, Connecticut, born in 1735.   They resided in Norwalk, Connecticut, until after the Revolution, and then removed to Ballston Spa,
New-York.   In February, 1775, he was appointed by the town of
Norwalk on a committee for the inspection of firearms, and was put
in charge of the gunpowder to see that it was properly preserved.   His
name is on the pay-roll of the Connecticut State Militia, in which he
held the rank of captain, serving in Danbury, Connecticut, at the time

of Tryon's Raid in April, 1777. In 1780 he was on a committee appointed by the Legislature to locate the boundaries belonging to a religious society. In a deed he is termed " gentleman." He died at Ballston Spa, New-York.

My great-grandfather, Clapp Raymond (2), son of Captain Clapp, resided in Dutchess County, New-York, and married on February 1, 1787, Sarah Dunning, who was born at Bethlehem, Litchfield County, Connecticut, near New Haven. Clapp Raymond died May 16, 1831. Sarah Dunning died at Poughkeepsie January 4, 1831.

My grandmother, Sarah Betsy Raymond (Potter), daughter of Clapp Raymond (2), was born at Patterson, New-York, August 27, 1792, and married February 28, 1811, Sheldon Potter, of Philadelphia. She died April 24, 1872, aged 80 years, and was buried in Philadelphia.

SUPPLEMENTARY RECORDS

OF

THE BENEDICTS.

The records of the Benedict branch of my family are so voluminous and well authenticated, so filled with instances of their patriotism worthy of being perpetuated, that I have prepared a brief extract.

The following officers and soldiers of the Revolution are the great-grandchildren and great-great-grandchildren of my great-great-great-great-great-grandfather, James Benedict, who was born in Southold, Long Island, 164–, and of his brothers, Thomas Benedict, Jr., John Benedict, Samuel Benedict, Daniel Benedict, all being my great-uncles of the same remove, and all born in the town of Southold, Long Island, between 164– and 165–.

COLONEL JOSEPH BENEDICT, born May 20, 1730; was appointed Captain Second Company, 4th New-York Continental Regiment, on June 28, 1775; Major, 1777; Lieutenant-Colonel, 1780.

LIEUTENANT EZRA BENEDICT, baptized May 27, 1746; appointed Ensign in May, 1777.   In 1780 he served as Ensign in Captain D. Olmstead's Company, near Horse Neck.

CAPTAIN BENJAMIN BENEDICT, born October 21, 1755. Served in the campaign of 1777 in the northern frontier, but most of his service was rendered on the " neutral ground " between the British army and New-York City and the American army. He was a minute-man and was a member of the guard over Major André during his trial and execution. Appointed Ensign May 4, 1780; Lieutenant, June 24, 1786; Captain, March 8, 1791.

ISAAC BENEDICT, born June 26, 1751. He was a Revolutionary War pensioner.

JOHN BENEDICT, born about 1740, was among the signers of the Revolutionary Pledge in 1775.

LEWIS BENEDICT served in Dellevan's Dragoons in 1780. He captured a British soldier who had accompanied the cow-boys that murdered a Mr. Pelham. Lewis took from the soldier a Queen's arm and a carved powder-horn, which are now in the possession of his descendants.

AMBROSE BENEDICT, a drummer, Seventh Company, Drake's 2d Regiment, Continental Army, 1777, served three years.

LIEUTENANT PETER BENEDICT was Second Lieutenant in the 3d New-York Continental Regiment in October, 1776; was appointed First Lieutenant November 1, 1776, in the 3d Continental Regiment. He is officially recorded as " a very good officer."

WILLIAM BENEDICT served in Colonel Wisler's Regiment, Continental Army.

JAMES BENEDICT, Revolutionary soldier and pensioner. He wintered at Valley Forge, and was on guard the day of André's execution.

DANIEL BENEDICT, soldier, died in the service, and was buried at Fort Ann, in 1779.

COLONEL JOSEPH BENEDICT served in Colonel Drake's 2d Regiment in 1775. In 1776 served at Crown Point, also at Fort Independence in 1777. Also Revolutionary Pensioner.

ENOCH BENEDICT, commissioned as Ensign in Drake's Regiment June 25, 1778.

GAMALIEL BENEDICT was Sergeant in Captain Olmstead's Company, Colonel Bebee's Regiment, in 1780, on the lines near Horse Neck.

NATHANIEL BENEDICT was a Revolutionary soldier.

WILLIAM BENEDICT was a soldier of the Revolution.

FRANCIS BENEDICT was a soldier of the Revolution.

CAPTAIN BENJAMIN BENEDICT, born September 27, 1740; Lieutenant in the Militia, and served as such in the Revolution.

ENSIGN WILLIAM BENEDICT, enlisted May 12, 1775; appointed Ensign in the Ninth Company, 5th Connecticut Regiment.

MOSES BENEDICT was a Revolutionary soldier.

AMOS BENEDICT, born November 30, 1756, was a Revolutionary pensioner.

MACAJAH BENEDICT, born November 2, 1762, was a Revolutionary pensioner.

ELISHA BENEDICT, born July 5, 1760, was a Revolutionary pensioner.

IRA BENEDICT, born January 13, 1763, militiaman stationed at West Point when General Washington crossed on his expedition against Lord Cornwallis.

ELIAS BENEDICT, born May 23, 1765, taken prisoner by the British in 1780.

JOHN BENEDICT, baptized 1765, was a Revolutionary pensioner.

LIEUTENANT LEMUEL BENEDICT, born August 10, 1734, was appointed Lieutenant in the Connecticut Line in 1776, and after the capture by the British of Forts Washington and Lee, in 1776, was left behind at Fishkill in charge of the sick of Colonel Bradley's regiment.

LIEUTENANT AARON BENEDICT, born January 17, 1745, was a Lieutenant in the Revolution, and served before Quebec, and placed on the pension-roll.

MATTHEW BENEDICT, born about 1733, was one of the persons taken prisoner in the British expedition to Danbury, and carried to

New-York.   He died in the Sugar House, a victim of British cruelty.
His heirs received from the State three hundred and thirty-four
pounds and ten shillings.

CAPTAIN NOBLE BENEDICT, born January 25, 1735; at the breaking
out of the Revolutionary War he raised a company of one hundred
soldiers in Fairfield County.   The original roll of this company is
on file at Hartford, Connecticut, and shows that five of his family
belonged to it.   He served at Ticonderoga, Montreal, and below Fort
St. John, all in 1775.   Taken prisoner in 1776 at Fort Washington,
on the Hudson.

ZADOCK BENEDICT, born 1737, suffered at the sacking of Danbury in
1777, and received from the State of Connecticut one hundred and
sixty-nine pounds and seventeen shillings for damages.

JONAH BENEDICT, born in 1747, was an active patriot.   Enlisted in
1775 as a Corporal.   Served at Ticonderoga and Fort St. John, and
was taken prisoner at Fort Washington in 1776.   Was confined in
the prison ship *Grosvenor*, and afterward removed to the Sugar
House and subjected to great hardships and cruelty.   When released
was considered to be at the point of death, and was carried to Danbury,
Connecticut, about two weeks before Danbury was burnt by the
British.   He and his old father Matthew, who was living in Jonah's
house, were taken out of their beds before daylight on Monday
morning, April 27, 1777, and tied to trees in his garden, while the
British troops set fire to his house.

ABIJAH BENEDICT was a Revolutionary soldier.

EBENEZER BENEDICT, born September 4, 1763, was a private in Captain David Olmstead's Company, Colonel Bebee's Regiment, Connecticut Line. Was honorably discharged in 1781, reënlisted in Major Shipman's Battalion, and discharged September 30, 1782. His entire service was on the lines near Horse Neck, and he frequently participated in skirmishes with De Lancey's Horse.

Of Nancy Benedict, born 1756, the daughter of Joseph and the great-granddaughter of John Benedict (my great-uncle, fifth remove), the following is related: In 1776, when General Howe advanced northward from New-York, she mounted a horse, followed the army, and witnessed the battle of White Plains. Her father, Joseph, lived near the "neutral ground," and had in his employ David Williams, who, when not engaged in military service in the militia on short enlistment, made the house of his employer his welcome home. Thus it happened that Williams was enjoying an agreeable tête-à-tête with Nancy in the fall of 1780, when she pointed out to him a small company of armed men approaching the village. They entered an inn near by, and Williams recognized Isaac Van Wart, John Paulding, and others. They set out together for Tarrytown, the special object of Williams being to reclaim the property of a neighbor, the widow Pelham, or avenge the death of her husband, killed the night before by a party of cow-boys.

At Tarrytown, Williams, Paulding, and his cousin Van Wart separated from their companions, taking the East Road, at an angle of which they concealed themselves, obtaining a north and west view of it for some distance.

The approach of Major André, his arrest, etc., followed. Congress granted Williams a medal, an annuity of $200, and a certain amount of confiscated lands. Nancy Benedict and Williams soon after married, and with the $1250 allowed for the lands purchased a farm.

Nancy received a pension until her death, which occurred in 1848, in the 92d year of her age, her husband David Williams having died in 1831.

It might be truly said that Nancy Williams caused indirectly the arrest of Major André.

REFERENCES.

The old Bailey Family Bible records from 1697, in my possession.

Benoni Bailey's Will, on probate at Fairfield, Connecticut.

The affidavit of Eli Westcott Bailey, in my possession.

The " Genealogy of the Benedicts in America."

The " History and Genealogies of the Potter Families in America."

A manuscript of old date, " Potter Family Record," which my grandmother, Sarah Betsy (Raymond) Potter, possessed at the time of her death. She was born in 1792, just one hundred years ago this year, 1892. This manuscript goes back to Robert Potter, who died in 1655. In my possession.

The " Greenes of Warwick" in colonial history. " Life of Major-General Nathaniel Greene," by George Washington Greene: see Appendix, first volume.

" Genealogical Dictionary of Rhode Island."

The " Genealogies of the Raymond Families of New England," also an old manuscript record of " The Raymond Family," which belonged to Sarah Betsy (Raymond) Potter. In my possession.

"The Ancient Historical Records of Norwalk, Connecticut," by Edwin Hall.

Other printed Colonial and Revolutionary Records, and private manuscripts.

THE ANCESTRY OF

Catherine Goddard Weaver (2), born Newport, Rhode Island, 1835, March 21, married September 1, 1857, Joseph Trowbridge Bailey (2), of Philadelphia, Pennsylvania.

HER ANCESTORS ARE:

Clement Weaver, 1590; William Spooner, about 1621; John Briggs, 1648; John Coggeshall, about 1591; William Freeborn, about 1600.

THE WEAVERS

OF NEWPORT, RHODE ISLAND.

Catherine Goddard Weaver (2), great-great-great-great-great-granddaughter of Clement Weaver, who was born approximative to 1590, died 1683, "nearly 100 years old." He landed in New England in 1650, and was a freeman of Newport, Rhode Island, in 1655. Deputy to General Assembly of Rhode Island in 1678.

He settled in Middletown, Rhode Island, three miles from Newport, and in Newport and Middletown his descendants in the direct line to Catherine Goddard Weaver (2) have lived for over 200 years. The old estate at Middletown is still in the possession of the family.

From the advent of Clement at Newport to the present period it may be said that each generation of the Weaver ancestors of Catherine Goddard Weaver (2) has proved active in the advancement and progress of Newport, Rhode Island.   In the annals of that city and Middletown, in town and state affairs, and Assemblies of Rhode Island, the names of her ancestors are of frequent recurrence.

They were Quakers, and lived up to the strict requirements of that religion, possessing the esteem and respect of the community.

Great-great-great-great-great-grandfather.

CLEMENT WEAVER, born about 1596, died 1683, married MARY FREE-
BORN, born 1627.   He was a freeman of Newport in 1655 ; Deputy
in 1678.

Great-great-great-great-grandfather.

THOMAS, died 1753, married MARY ———— ; Deputy to the General
Assembly of Rhode Island 1696, 1710, 1715, 1721, 1722, 1723, and
one of the Proprietors of Common Lands, 1702.

Great-great-great-grandfather.

BENJAMIN, died 1754, married HANNAH COGGESHALL, died 1763.

Great-great-grandfather.

THOMAS, born May 1, 1718, died 1802, married RUTH ————.

Great-grandfather.

PERRY, born May 5, 1755, died June 27, 1827, married CATHERINE
GODDARD (1), born April 10, 1757, died March 24, 1816.

Grandfather.

BENJAMIN, born Newport March 4 1781, married HANNAH SPOONER
BRIGGS, born Newport January, 1783, died October 9, 1847; mem-

ber of Newport Artillery, 1814; member of General Assembly of
Newport, Rhode Island, 1819; delegate to form the Constitution of
Rhode Island in 1834; reëlected to General Assembly in 1837 and
served until 1843; Presidential Elector, 1844; Senator Rhode Island
Assembly, 1845–46, and held many other important positions; died
May 11, 1863.

Father.

JOSEPH BRIGGS WEAVER, born November 7, 1810, died Newport,
Rhode Island, January 20, 1873, married June 9, 1833, ABBY DYER
(MARSH) WEAVER, born July 27, 1811, died Providence, Rhode
Island, buried Newport, Rhode Island, May 16, 1878, daughter of
BENJAMIN MARSH and FANNY (PETERSON) MARSH, of Newport,
Rhode Island. Often elected to General Assembly, Rhode Island,
and City Councils of Newport.

Their daughter.

CATHERINE GODDARD WEAVER (2), born March 21, 1835, Newport,
Rhode Island.

THE SPOONERS,

ORIGINALLY OF DARTMOUTH, MASSACHUSETTS,

AFTERWARDS OF NEWPORT, RHODE ISLAND.

WILLIAM SPOONER, great-great-great-great-great-grandfather of
CATHERINE GODDARD WEAVER (2), arrived in New Plymouth Settlement, Massachusetts, in 1637, aged at that time about 16 years. He
probably came over with ANN SPOONER and THOMAS SPOONER, from
Leyden, Holland, who arrived the same year. Married March 18,
1652, HANNAH PRATT. Will dated March, 1683.

Great-great-great-great-grandfather.

SAMUEL SPOONER, born Dartmouth, Massachusetts, January 14, 1655, died 1739, married EXPERIENCE WING, born August 4, 1668, living in September, 1731.

Great-great-great-grandmother.

BEULAH SPOONER, born Dartmouth, Massachusetts, January 27, 1705, married JOHN SPOONER.

Great-great-grandfather.

WING SPOONER, born Newport, Rhode Island, December 30, 17—, died prior to 1774, married DEBORAH CHURCH March 9 1729. Held various offices in city of Newport for years.

Great-grandmother.

MARY SPOONER, born Newport, Rhode Island, December 28, 1747, died April 2, 1830, married July 14, 1774, JOSEPH BRIGGS, born June 7, 1749, died October 5, 1830.

Grandmother.

HANNAH BRIGGS, born Newport, Rhode Island, January 4, 1783, died October 19, 1847, married October 29, 1809, BENJAMIN WEAVER, born Newport, Rhode Island, March 4, 1781, died May 11, 1863.

Father.

JOSEPH BRIGGS WEAVER, born Newport November 7, 1810, was the father of CATHERINE GODDARD WEAVER (2).

THE BRIGGS

OF NEWPORT, RHODE ISLAND.

CATHERINE GODDARD WEAVER (2) is the great-great-great-great-great-granddaughter of JOHN BRIGGS, who was admitted freeman of Newport, Rhode Island, in 1648.

Also the great-granddaughter of Joseph Briggs, who was born June 9, 1749, died October 5, 1830; was in the Privateer Service and a soldier in the Continental Army, War of the Revolution, Captain Jeremiah Olney's Fourth Company, Colonel Hitchcock's Regiment, Army of Observation, raised in Providence, Rhode Island, May, 1775, to December 31, 1775. It is recorded that he rendered considerable additional service.

THE COGGESHALLS

OF NEWPORT, RHODE ISLAND.

JOHN COGGESHALL, the great-great-great-great-great-great-grandfather of Catherine Goddard Weaver (2), was descended from an ancient family of Essex, England, born in 1591, and arrived in Boston, New England, in the ship *Lyon*, Captain Pierce, September 16, 1632, and admitted a freeman of that town November 6 the same year; 1634, contributed money toward building a sea fort; September 3, 1634, chosen one of the overseers of powder, shot, etc.; 1636, on committee to make tax rates for Massachusetts towns. On the formation of the city government of Boston, he was elected a member of the First Board of Selectmen instituted in that town, and also represented the town in the Colonial

Assembly of Massachusetts for 1634, 1635, and 1636, and the spring session of 1637. That same year he was "Disfranchised for conscience towards God," and with others who sought religious liberty he left Boston, and on March 7, 1637, John Coggeshall, with seventeen others, landed and established themselves permanently on the island of Aquidneck, later called by the colonists Rhode Island. The lands they occupied were purchased from the. Indian Sachems Miantonomy and Canonicus, November 22, 1639, on part of which is situated the city of Newport, Rhode Island.   These eighteen pioneers were the first to arrive and settle in Rhode Island, and were the founders of that portion of the present State and the city of Newport, Rhode Island.

They soon entered into a body politic, and the following is an extract from that compact :

"We, whose names are underwritten, do swear, solemnly, in the presence of the Great Jehovah, to incorporate ourselves into a body politic ; and He shall help us,— will submit our persons, lives, and estates, unto the Lord Jesus Christ, the King of kings, and Lord of lords ; and to all those perfect laws of his, given us in his most holy word of truth, to be guided and judged thereby."

He was Assistant in 1640, 1641, 1642, 1643, and 1644; Corporal in 1644; Moderator in 1647, and the first President of the Colony of Rhode Island, and died November 27, 1647, and was buried on his own land.

Joshua Coggeshall, great-great-great-great-great-grandfather of Catherine Goddard Weaver (2), was born 1623, married December 2, 1652, Joan West, born 1631, died April 24, 1676.

He embraced Quakerism, and for which, when in Plymouth Colony, he was seized, put in jail, and his horse taken from him.

He was Deputy to the General Assembly of Rhode Island in 1664, 1666, 1667, 1668, 1670, 1671, 1672 ; Assistant, 1669, 1670, 1672, 1673,

1674, 1675, 1676; was appointed in May 7, 1673, to treat with King Philip and other Indian Sachems; was a member of Court Martial in trial of Indians, August 24, 1676. He died May 1, 1688.

Great-great-great-great-great-great-grandfather.

JOHN COGGESHALL, born 1591, died Nov. 27, 1647, married MARY
———, born 1604, died Nov. 8, 1684.

Great-great-great-great-great-grandfather.

JOSHUA, born 1623, died May 1, 1688, married JOAN WEST, born 1631, died April 24, 1676.

Great-great-great-great-grandfather.

JOHN COGGESHALL, born Dec. 1659, died May 1, 1727, married MARY STANTON, born June 4, 1668, died May 11, 1747, daughter JOHN and MARY (HARNDEL) STANTON.

Great-great-great-grandmother.

HANNAH COGGESHALL, died 1763, married BENJAMIN WEAVER (3), died 1754, both of Newport, Rhode Island.

Great-great-grandfather.

THOMAS WEAVER (4), born May 1, 1718, died 1802, married RUTH
———.

Great-grandfather.

PERRY WEAVER, born May 5, 1755, died June 27, 1827, married CATHERINE GODDARD (1), born April 10, 1757, died March 24, 1816.

Grandfather.

BENJAMIN WEAVER (4), born March 4, 1781, died May 11, 1863, married HANNAH BRIGGS, born Jan. 4, 1783, died Oct. 9, 1847, daughter of JOSEPH and MARY (SPOONER) BRIGGS.

Father.

JOSEPH BRIGGS WEAVER, born Nov. 7, 1810, died January 20, 1873, married June 9, 1833, ABBY (DYER) MARSH, born July 27, 1811, died May 16, 1878.

All of Newport, Rhode Island.

THE FREEBORNS

OF NEWPORT, RHODE ISLAND.

WILLIAM FREEBORN was one of that party who, with John Coggeshall and sixteen others, were the first settlers of Rhode Island, March, 1637, and founders of the city of Newport, Rhode Island.   Catherine Goddard Weaver (2) is his great-great-great-great-great-great-grand-daughter.

REFERENCES.

"Genealogical Dictionary of Rhode Island."   Weavers, Coggeshalls, Freeborn, Briggs.

"Records of William Spooner, Plymouth, Massachusetts, and his Descendants," by Thomas Spooner.   Full records from William Spooner, 1630, to Catherine Goddard (Weaver) (2) Bailey, 1892.   Briggs also. Weavers also.

Will of Thomas Weaver, of Middletown, Rhode Island, dated August 1, 1794, proved June 2, 1802.

"Spirit of '76 in Rhode Island" (page 20), by Benjamin Colwell, 1850.   Briggs.

7

"History of Rhode Island and Newport," by Rev. Edward Peterson, page 20.

A verified pedigree of the Coggeshalls and Weavers, kindly furnished to me by Mr. John Osborne Austin, of Providence, Rhode Island, author of "The Genealogical Dictionary of Rhode Island," and now in my possession.

JOSEPH TROWBRIDGE BAILEY (2).

APPENDIX.

JOSEPH TROWBRIDGE BAILEY (1), second marriage, August 29, 1843, MARIE LOUISE BARRY, of New-York City, born July 8, 1820, died March 21, 1882. Had four children.

Their children.

1. MARIE LOUISE, born October 17, 1846, died April 5, 1881, married RICHARD T. JONES, died June 6, 1869. No children.
2. LUCY, born July 10, 1848, died in Paris, France, October 22, 1872, unmarried.
3. MEREDITH (1), born May 11, 1850, first marriage, October 29, 1873, ANNA CARVER, daughter of JEREMIAH MAYBURRY and EMMA (HARBERT) BROOKS, of Philadelphia; one child: MEREDITH (2), born November 28, 1875. Second marriage, November 3, 1880, HENRIETTA HORSTMANN, daughter of JOSEPH and LIVINIA (HORSTMANN) PATTERSON, of Philadelphia; one child: CURTIS PATTERSON, born September 15, 1881.
4. JOSEPHINE, born May 2, 1854.

———

ELI WESTCOTT BAILEY, second son of MAJOR and LUCY (BENEDICT) BAILEY, born February 21, 1809, at Bloomingburg, Sullivan County, New-York, only brother of JOSEPH TROWBRIDGE BAILEY (1), married on June 21, 1834, at Philadelphia, by the Rt. Rev. William White, Episcopal Bishop of Pennsylvania, ESTHER ANN WHITNEY. Had six children.

Their children.

1. MARY WHITNEY, born April 17, 1835, married June 3, 1857, HERBERT RAY CLARK, of New-York, now resident in Jersey City, New Jersey; 2. FRANCIS HAYES, born January 8, 1838, died February 10, 1863; 3. BENJAMIN NORMAN, born October 10, 1840; 4. JOSEPH T., born May 6, 1843, died May 31, 1864; 5. WESTCOTT, born August 16, 1846; 6. JULIA, born December 6, 1848. All born in Philadelphia.

———

MAJOR and LUCY (BENEDICT) BAILEY had two daughters:

MARY WHITE, born October 20, 1814, married December 7, 1854, JAMES R. BALDING, died February 27, 1872. No children. Mrs. BALDING resides in Philadelphia. HANNAH, born December 22, 1816, died January, 1877, married February 6, 1844, HECTOR MORISON, of New-York, died 1876. Had four children.

Their children.

1. LUCY, born November 13, 1844, died June 1, 1850; 2. MARY, born March 12, 1848, married June 10, 1869, EDWARD STELLE BROWNSON ; 3. ROBERT STRATTON, born November 24, 1849, married LOUISE VAN BERGEN; 4. JOSEPH BAILEY, born May 12, 1854. All of Brooklyn, New-York.

———

JOSEPH BRIGGS and ABBY (DYER) MARSH WEAVER had four children.

Their children.

1. CATHERINE GODDARD WEAVER (2), whose ancestry has been given.

2. BENJAMIN MARSH, born August 10, 1837, at Newport, Rhode Island, married MARY M. WARD, of Newark, New Jersey. No children.

3. ANN LAWTON, born April 4, 1845, at Newport, Rhode Island, married September 8, 1869, PHILIP STEPHEN (1) CHASE,* born November 3, 1843, son of PHILIP BRIGGS and SARAH EARL (COOK) CHASE, Portsmouth, Rhode Island. Their children: JOSEPH WEAVER, born October 14, 1872, died April 19, 1889; ABBY MARSH, born May 10, 1875; ANNIE, born February 21, 1877; PHILIP STEPHEN (2), born May 17, 1881. All of Providence, Rhode Island.

4. CLEMENT WEAVER, born March 26, 1848, at Newport, Rhode Island, married November 5, 1874, CAROLINE,† born January 21, 1851, daughter of HENRY and CAROLINE (WORRELL) SLOAN, of Philadelphia. Their children: ELIZABETH SLOAN, born Philadelphia, December 30, 1876; JOSEPH BRIGGS, born Philadelphia, June 19, 1880.

———

HENRY AUGUSTUS BURROUGHS, born Philadelphia, March 10, 1856, died March 1, 1882, was great-great-great-great-grandson of JOHN BURROUGHS, born in 1612, who settled first in Salem, Massachusetts, and later at Newtown, Long Island, where he died in 1673; his son, JOHN, born Newtown, 1665, died 1699; his son, JOHN, born 1684, died in 1772, at Ewing, Old Huntington County, New Jersey; his son, JOSEPH, born 1725, died 1798; his son, JOHN, born Trenton, 1759, died 1817; his son, HORATIO NELSON (1), born June 28, 1812, married July, 1854, CAROLINE, born September 4, 1817, daughter of SAMUEL AUGUSTUS and RHODA ANN (FULLER) MITCHELL; their only child, HENRY AUGUSTUS BURROUGHS, who was also great-great-great-great-great-great-grandson of EDWARD FULLER, one of the company who arrived in the *Mayflower,* and landed at Plymouth in 1620. EDWARD, SAMUEL, JOHN, THOMAS, THOMAS OLIVER and THOMAS FULLER.

* Philip S. Chase, Second Lieutenant, served in War of Rebellion, Battery F, 1st Rhode Island Artillery, from 1861 to 1865; was with Burnside, Coast Division, and in North Carolina until October, 1863; was with the Eighteenth Army Corps of the James in Virginia during the Campaign of 1864. Since the war was Captain and Adjutant 1st Light Infantry Regiment, Rhode Island; Lieutenant-Colonel and Assistant Adjutant-General Brigade Rhode Island Militia from June, 1879, to March 21, 1892. Representative to General Assembly from Portsmouth, Rhode Island, 1867–1868.

† Great-great-great-great-granddaughter of John Worrell, from Berkshire, England, 1682. His name is on a deed of land granted by William Penn. Member of Pennsylvania Assembly, 1716. Isaiah Worrell was her great-great-grandfather. He and his five sons were Quakers, joined the Revolutionary army, and were read out of Quaker meeting. John Hawley Worrell was her great-grandfather, also great-great-great-niece of Major-General Isaac Worrell, Revolutionary officer. Grandfather was William Worrell.

The family have resided in the immediate vicinity of Philadelphia since 1682.

Great-great-grandson of Doctor OLIVER FULLER, graduate of Yale, Class 1762, born September 30, 1742, died March 9, 1817; born in East Haddam, Connecticut; located in Kent, Connecticut; married ALICE, daughter of Colonel JOHN RANSOM, died in Kent, Connecticut; Captain in the Continental army, War of the Revolution.

HORATIO NELSON BURROUGHS (1) is a successful merchant, and President of the Commonwealth National Bank of Philadelphia.

The ancestral records of Henry Augustus Burroughs show that on both sides of his family his grandfathers for many generations were highly educated men; a number were graduates of Yale College, New Haven, and attained eminence in professional pursuits. His records are obtained from "The Genealogy of Early Settlers in Trenton and Ewing, Old Huntington County, New Jersey," by Rev. Eli F. Cooley, of Trenton. Manuscript in possession of Horatio Nelson Burroughs (1), Philadelphia. Complete records of Fuller family in possession of Mrs. Effingham (Burroughs) Perot, Philadelphia.

———

EDMUND BRANDT AYMAR, born September 7, 1858.

There are but few records in this country of the Aymars prior to November 18, 1731. Family traditions and brief memoranda indicate that they left their native province, Dauphine, France, on the revocation of the " Edict of Nantes," 1685, in the reign of Louis XIV.

It is said they fled in such haste that the meat was left roasting before the fire and the bread baking in the oven. They escaped by way of Germany, afterward going to England. An incident in their passage across the North Sea forms the subject of Edwin White's beautiful picture, the " Evening Hymn of the Huguenot Refugees."

In England they found no resting-place, so embarked for New-York; but owing to the vessel becoming disabled in a storm, they were compelled to stop at the island of New Providence for repairs. Tempted by the beauty of the scenery and the mildness of the climate, they remained for a while, occupying an estate which they named " Bon Dieu." Not being satisfied, as there was no place of worship in accordance with their language and faith, they again sailed for New-York, and among the records of the church " Du Esprit " (the French Protestant Episcopal Church in Twenty-second Street) we find a baptismal notice of " Marie Aymar," daughter of John (or Jean) Aymar and Francaise Belon, his wife. Daniel was the first born in this country, after the arrival of the family in New-York.

1. JEAN AYMAR married FRANCAISE BELON; 2. DANIEL, born November 28, 1733, died 1770. married ANN MAGDELAINE, daughter of FRANCIS and HANNAH ———, in the year 1755; 3. JOHN D., born January 28, 1758, married, first, JANE LEGARE, second, JUDITH QUEREAU third, ELIZABETH QUEREAU: the Quereaus were in New-York in 1729; 4. BENJAMIN, the second son of JOHN D. AYMAR and JUDITH QUEREAU, born December 17, 1791, died March 16, 1876, married ELIZABETH, daughter of COURTLANDT VAN BUREN; 5. EDMUND BRANDT (1), son of BENJAMIN and ELIZABETH VAN BUREN, had one child, EDMUND BRANDT (2), who married EMILIE (BAILEY) BURROUGHS; COURTLANDT VAN BUREN of New-York was his great-grandfather. ———

AMY (THOMSON) BAILEY, born Philadelphia, October 12, 1862, daughter of ALEXANDER HAMILTON and CAROLINE MACKEY (WHITE) THOMSON, of Philadelphia; great-great-great-granddaughter of WILLIAM FLOYD (1734–1821), Member of Congress and signer of Declaration of Independence, and Colonel of 1st Regiment Suffolk County Militia, New-York, 1775; great-

great-granddaughter of Major and Brevet Lieutenant-Colonel BENJAMIN TALLMADGE (1754–1835), Captain 1776, Major in Sheldon's Light Dragoons 1774; conducted "Secret Service" for commander-in-chief; captured Fort George, Long Island, November 21, 1780, and received special notice of Congress; Lieutenant-Colonel by brevet, 1783.

FREDERICK SAMUEL TALLMADGE, uncle, President of the New-York Society, "Sons of the Revolution," this date, 1892.

JEAN THÉODULE FRANCISQUE LOUIS, COMTE DE SIBOUR.

DE BOURBON
Louis IX. (Saint Louis*)
King of France,
born 1215.
His Son
Robert de France
Comte de Clermont, etc.
His Son
Louis (I.),
Duc de Bourbon, etc.
His Son

DE SALLMARD.
Seigneurs de Ressiz et de Montfort.
A. D. 1330.
Bernard,
Comte de Sallmard.
His Son

Jacques de Bourbon (I.),
Duc de Bourbon, Comte de
la Marche, etc.
His Son
Jean de Bourbon (I.),
Comte de la Marche, etc.
His Son

Humbert.
His Son
Guilhaume.
His Son
Albert.
His Son
Bertrand, married May 21, 1469, Jeanne de Bourbon de Carenci,

Jean de Bourbon (II.),
Seigneur de Carenci en Arrois, de
Buquoi de l'Ecluse et de Duisant,
Chamberlain of Charles VI.
His Daughter

Their Son
Claude,
Comte de Sallmard, Seigneur de Ressiz et de Montfort.

DE SIBOUR.
A. D. 1500.
Antoine,
Comte de Sibour.
His Son
Antoine.
His Son
Jean.
His Son
Esprit.
His Son
Jean François.
His Son
François.
His Son
Jean Claude.
His Son
Jean François.
His Son
Jean Joseph François.
His Son

Claude.
His Son
Godfroy.
His Son
Godfroy.
His Son
Jean.
His Son
Louis.
His Son
Philippe.
His Son
Raymond.
His Son
Raymond.
His Daughter

Jean Batiste Joseph, married June 1, 1813, Pauline, Comtesse de Sallmard.

Their Son
Jean Antonin Gabriel.
His Son
Jean Théodule Francisque Louis.

* Descended from Hughes Capet, First King of France, A. D. 987–996.

DE SIBOUR, origin Prussian, removed in A. D. 1500 to Comtat Venaissin, now Vaucluse, France, and resided on their estate "Loupillier," which is now owned by LOUIS DE SIBOUR. The name in early manuscripts, previous to 1650, was spelled "Sibourd" or "Sibourg." In all official documents since that date the name is written SIBOUR, but frequently, from individual preference, the "g" has been retained.

It is a task of magnitude to attempt any history of the family. The de Sibours and de Sallmards, and families into which they married, were all noble. Reference is therefore made herein to grandfather and great-grandfather only.

Great-grandfather.

JEAN JOSEPH FRANÇOIS, born October 3, 1734, Carpentras, France, died July 19, 1819, married MARIE FRANÇOIS DE LA SELLE, June 5, 1765, was Procureur du Saint Siège, Conseiller du Roi, Lieutenant Général de la Sénéchaussée de Carpentras, First Consul of Comtat Venaissin, President of the Reverend Apostolic Chamber, Chevalier of the Order of the Fleur de Lys.

Grandfather.

JEAN BATISTE JOSEPH, born June 25, 1767, Carpentras, died July 19, 1843, married PAULINE, Comtesse DE SALLMARD, daughter of RAYMOND, Comte DE SALLMARD, Seigneur de Ressiz et de Montfort, one of the most ancient families of Dauphiné, was Procureur du Saint Siège, Breveté de l'Ordre du Fleur de Lys, Chevalier Légion d'Honneur, Mayor of Monteux, Captain of Second Company "Mousquetaires Nobles d'Ordonnance" (King's Body-guard), equerry to the king, served in various campaigns, 24 years, received from Louis XVIII. a personally signed letter of acknowledgment of his fidelity and valuable services, refused to swear allegiance to Napoleon I., and on the Restoration raised the second Royal Bourbon flag which was floated over a French city, was restored by the king to his former honors.

Father.

JEAN ANTONIN GABRIEL, VICOMTE, second son of JEAN BATISTE JOSEPH, born August 7 1821, Carpentras, died August 7, 1885, married MARY LOUISE JOHNSON, was in consular service of France till his death.

Their son.

JEAN THÉODULE FRANCISQUE LOUIS, COMTE, born March 19, 1865, inherited title "Vicomte" on death of father, 1885, that of "Comte" from uncle, JOSEPH LOUIS ANTOINE, who was first son of JEAN BATISTE JOSEPH, and who died 1889, unmarried.

Louis de Sibour is a lineal descendant of the Bourbons of France; his great-grandmother (10th) was Jeanne de Bourbon de Carenci. He is the only member of the family de Sibour resident in France, excepting his son, Louis Blaise (Vicomte), born December 26, 1891.

GRANT OF ARMS. DE SIBOUR. D'azur à trois bandes d'or, acc. en chef d'une étoile du même et en p. de trois bes. d'arg. en point; l'écu timbré d'un casque de profil, orné de ses lambrequins.
A count's coronet has been sometimes used instead of the helmet and plumes.

A collection of many hundreds of manuscripts, inherited by Louis de Sibour, contains a complete history of the family. These papers, entirely appertaining to the de Sibour family, are
most interesting. They comprise certificates of birth, death, contracts of marriage, wills, and many
letters of social correspondence; about one half are official documents from kings, princes, popes,
and many minor dignitaries; ecclesiastical appointments, law, military commissions of all ranks
to that of commandant, military instructions to those in service, brevets of decorations, reconfir-
mation of titles after the Revolution, many letters of acknowledgment for services rendered to
the kingdom. These documents are written in French, Italian, or Latin, embracing a period
from 1535 to 1820.

It is from a personal perusal of a portion of this remarkable collection of manuscripts that I
have prepared the above sketch of the de Sibour family.

N. B. Since compiling the foregoing record, I find in the Bibliothèque Nationale de France,
Paris, the following authority, published under Royal Sanction, which contains a very complete,
history of the families de Sibour, de Sallmard, and their relation to the House of Bourbon.

This work, "Nobiliaire Universel de France, par M. de Saint-Allais, avec privilege du Roi
avant la Révolution."—Volume II, pages 154, 155, 156, 157.   Volume VIII, pages 277, 278,
279, 280, verifies completely my compilation from the manuscripts.